You'll Never Believe This!

Written by
John Townsend

Some people talk about the weather a lot. They moan if it gets too hot or wet, or cold or windy. If it gets very stormy or snowy, the weather affects us all.

But you'll never believe just how scary the weather can be at times. Now and again it turns wild, weird and wacky.

Get ready to be amazed …

It Looks Like Rain

We all know what rain is. It is drops of water falling from the clouds. Wrong! That's *usually* true – but not always. Now and again, the rain is alive.

At a boat race in Mexico in 1968, an odd thing happened. The sky grew dark. People looked up at the clouds in shock. The rain was white. It was raining live maggots! Fat, wriggly maggots over 2cm long fell on the crowds.

In 2014 a storm began to blow in Sri Lanka. People in the town of Chilaw took shelter from the rain, but next came heavy splats on the roofs. They looked up to see live fish falling from the sky. Two years before, it had rained down prawns in the same country.

In fact, 'fish rain' can happen around the world. The UK has been rained on by fish as well.

Can you believe it?

This is a news story from 2010 in Australia.

Town 326 miles from river hit by raining fish

People in a small desert town in Australia had to shelter for two days – from live fish raining from the sky. Weather experts believe the fish were sucked up from a river in a storm. Strong winds blew the fish – they were small perch – high into the sky. They later dropped to Earth in a fishy downpour.

A witness said, "I've often seen fish in water, but never in the sky. What if anything bigger falls from the clouds next time? If it's crocodiles – that would be really scary!"

Have you heard the saying 'it's raining cats and dogs'? Be warned – it could happen!

What is going on?

Strong, twisting winds are to blame. They are called waterspouts.

A waterspout is a column of cloud-filled wind. The air inside the column spins round and round very quickly. It twists down from a storm cloud and skims over water. Any small creature near the surface of the water could be dragged up into the sky.

Waterspouts are like mini tornadoes, but they are weaker. They can still be dangerous to swimmers and boats. Planes flying near waterspouts can be thrown off-course by the swirling winds.

When a waterspout moves from the water and crosses land, it gets weaker. Anything it dragged up from the water can then fall back to Earth.

All kinds of things can fall on you. Jellyfish and seaweed have rained on streets in the UK, and so have frogs, toads and tadpoles.

A waterspout can also suck up pond water. It may lift everything in the pond as well. When it falls again, it doesn't just rain. You could get covered in frogs.

You won't just get soaked ... but croaked!

It can be bad news for birds in poor weather. Heavy storms can send flocks of birds spinning to the ground.

When lightning strikes birds in the clouds, they will fall from the sky. Then it rains birds and feathers.

This is a news story from Canada in 1932.

The Day it Rained Geese

On 22nd April it rained geese in Elgin. A large flock of geese was flying off to summer nesting grounds when lightning struck. 52 geese fell from the sky onto the small town. People had to dodge the falling birds. But their goose was cooked! Sizzling birds landed at their feet. People ran to pick up the ready-cooked dinners around the town. They thought Christmas had come early!

Fire from the sky

Did you know?

- ✓ Lightning is a powerful burst of electricity during a thunderstorm.

- ✓ Bolts of lightning strike the Earth every second.

- ✓ Lightning strikes usually last only one or two millionths of a second.

- ✓ Lightning contains millions of volts of electricity.

- ✓ Thunder is the sound caused by lightning.

- ✓ The temperature of lightning is around 20,000 degrees celsius. That's hot!

Can you believe it?

Roy Sullivan was a park ranger in the USA. He was struck by lightning seven times between 1942 and 1977. That's unlucky!

He survived each zap, but he lost a toenail, had his legs burnt and his chest scorched. His eyebrows burnt off in 1969 and his hair went up in flames – twice!

Raining balls of ice

When rain freezes as it falls, look out! You may think hailstones are just small lumps of ice, but now and again they can be huge. Some of the largest hailstones have caused very serious damage.

A car damaged by hailstones

Bigger than a baseball!

Can you believe it?

The biggest ever hailstones fell in Bangladesh. Each hailstone weighed over one kilogramme. That's the same weight as a bag of sugar!

Imagine hundreds of bags of sugar falling from the sky at once. The roofs of many buildings were destroyed.

For the record

Here are some of the most extreme weather events recorded:

* Lowest temperature
  -89.2° centigrade (July 1983)
  Vostok, Antarctica

* Highest temperature
  56.7° centigrade (July 1913)
  Furnace Creek, California, USA

Near Furance Creek, California

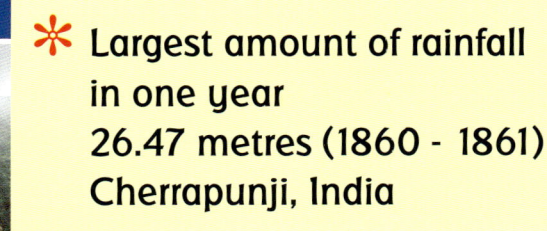

* Largest amount of rainfall in one year
  26.47 metres (1860 - 1861)
  Cherrapunji, India

* Fastest gust of wind
  253 mph (April 1996)
  Barrow Island, Australia

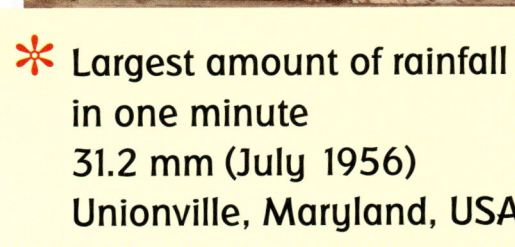

* Largest amount of rainfall in one minute
  31.2 mm (July 1956)
  Unionville, Maryland, USA

So next time someone moans about the weather, you can tell them it could be a lot worse! All you have to say is, "You'll never believe this ... "

They might be amazed by what you tell them.